Frank and the Evil Crows

Om KIDZ
An imprint of Om Books International

Om Books International

Reprinted in 2023

Corporate & Editorial Office
A-12, Sector 64, Noida 201 301
Uttar Pradesh, India
Phone: +91 120 477 4100
Email: editorial@ombooks.com
Website: www.ombooksinternational.com

Sales Office
107, Ansari Road, Darya Ganj
New Delhi 110 002, India
Phone: +91 11 4000 9000
Email: sales@ombooks.com
Website: www.ombooks.com

ISBN: 978-93-52760-24-4

Printed in India

10 9 8 7 6 5 4 3 2

Frank and the Evil Crows

Paste your photograph here

My name is

Frank works at a farm. He wakes up **early every** morning. He **eats** an **egg** and goes to the **farm.** He **earns** money by selling his crops.

A **family** of crows also lives on the **farm.** The **evil** crows trouble **Frank every** day. They love to **eat** the crops.

One day, **Frank forgets** to set his alarm clock. He does not wake up **early.** He reaches the **farm** a **few** minutes late.

When **Frank enters** the **farm,** he is shocked!

Eight crows are busy pulling out the crops **from** the **earth.** He runs towards them.

The crows **fly** away in **fear.** **Frank's face falls.** A lot of his grains are **eaten.**

Frank has to **find** a way
to stop the crows. But **first,**
he must **fix** his **farm.**
This will not be **easy.**

Four days later, **Frank** **finishes fixing** his **farm**.

Now he has to **find** a way to **frighten** the birds.

All of a sudden, **Frank** has

an **excellent** little idea.

That **evening, Frank** decides

to make a scarecrow.

What a **fantastic** idea!

Frank finds an old shirt and a pair of pants. He stuffs them both **full** of hay.

Then, he takes an **empty** pot.

He draws a **face** on it. It has **eyes** and **ears** and **everything else.**

Frank fits all the parts together. In the **end,** it becomes a huge, scary scarecrow!

To **Frank,** the scarecrow looks **friendly enough.**

But it is **four feet** tall. To the crows, it looks like an **enemy.**

The crows take one look at the scarecrow and **freeze** in **fear.**

They are too afraid to
even stand in **front** of it.

The crows never **ever fly** into **Frank's farm** again. **Frank finally** saves his **farm from** the crows, **forever.**

Know your words

Naming words

Frank
farm
family
face
feet
egg
earth
evening
eyes
ears
enemy

Describing words

few
first
front
fantastic
full
friendly
four
freeze
early
every
evil
eight
easy
excellent
empty

Doing words

forgets
fly
falls
find
fixing
finishes
frighten
fits
freeze
eats
earns
enters

Sight words

eaten
from
end
enough
else
finally
ever
even

Join the dots and find out what the crows are afraid of.

Find the words from the word search.
Use the clue box given below.

O	E	Z	W	F	A	H	D
O	V	T	Z	N	T	S	E
E	E	I	F	R	F	F	R
G	N	U	A	A	A	E	D
G	I	E	R	V	M	C	L
D	N	O	M	R	I	F	R
I	G	G	A	T	L	U	B
Y	E	F	B	O	Y	I	J

FARMER
EGG
FARM
EARTH
FAMILY
EVENING

Help Frank reach the scarecrow.